DINOSAURS

Written by
Steve Pollock

Illustrated by
**John Blackman, Norma Burgin, Ray Burrows, Angelika Elsebach,
David Holmes, Josephine Martin, Mark Peppé**

Designed by
Anthony Bussey

Edited by
Jenny Vaughan

Scientific consultant
Dr Angela Milner

CONTENTS

BBC

About this book

This book is all about dinosaurs and how they lived.

Dinosaurs ruled the land for over 160 million years. Then, 65 million years ago, they became extinct. (That means they died out.) We can never be sure how they lived. So we must guess.

It helps us to guess if we look at the way animals live today. That is why there are pictures in this book that show animals you may already know. These might help you understand more about the dinosaurs.

If you think you already know a lot about dinosaurs, try this quiz.

Dinosaur quiz

Here are some questions people often ask about dinosaurs. The answers can be found all through this book – and on pages 46–47.
Were all dinosaurs big?
Could dinosaurs swim or fly?
Are there any dinosaurs alive now?
Has anyone seen a live dinosaur?
Were all dinosaurs stupid?
Were they slow and lumbering?
Were any dinosaurs colourful?
Were dinosaurs warm blooded, like us, or cold blooded, like reptiles now?
Were they bound to become extinct?

Dinosaur profiles

In the book, there are some profiles of dinosaurs. For each one, there is a box of information like the one below. You will need to use the key to help you understand all the information.

There will be a picture to help you see the size of the dinosaur.

The dinosaur is **bird-hipped**.

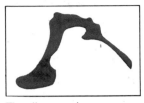

The dinosaur is **lizard-hipped**.

DINOSAUR FACTFILE

Bird-hipped   Plants   Woody land

Try-serra-tops

70–65 million years ago

The dinosaur ate plants (it was **herbivorous**).

The dinosaur ate other animals (it was **carnivorous**).

The dinosaur ate both plants and animals (it was **omnivorous**).

The dinosaur lived in swampy land.

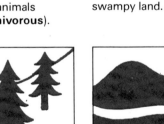

The dinosaur lived in woody land.

The dinosaur lived in open land.

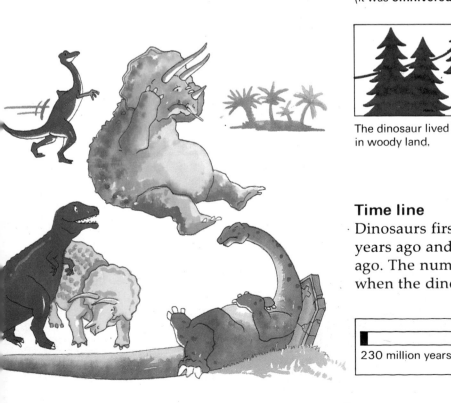

Time line

Dinosaurs first appeared 230 million years ago and died out 65 million years ago. The number on the time line shows when the dinosaurs lived.

230 million years ago   65 million years ago

What was a dinosaur?

Look at the picture. You will see many different animals. Some were alive millions of years ago. Others are alive today. Only two of them are dinosaurs. Which are they?

If you are not sure about which animals are dinosaurs, read the next page. The answers are upside-down at the bottom. Do you think everything that is extinct is a dinosaur?

pterosaur

Iguanodon

ostrich

mammoth

monitor lizard

plesiosaur

Diplodocus

tortoise

Dinosaur legs

The reptiles alive today are the lizards, snakes, tortoises and turtles, crocodiles and alligators. Dinosaurs were reptiles too – but they were different from the reptiles we see today. In what way?

Dinosaurs had legs attached to their body like this:

These legs were attached to their bodies more like mammals than other reptiles. This shows dinosaurs were land animals. They could move quickly, but none of them could fly or swim.

Other reptiles' legs are different. They are attached to their body like this:

Dinosaur hips

Scientists are interested in dinosaur hip bones.

They have split dinosaurs into two groups, depending on what kind of hips they had.

This is the hip of a *lizard-hipped* dinosaur (*saurischia*).

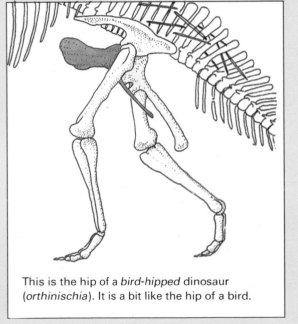

This is the hip of a *bird-hipped* dinosaur (*orthinischia*). It is a bit like the hip of a bird.

The dinosaur story

The dinosaur story began in 1822.

A woman called Mary Ann Mantell was walking past a quarry in Sussex. There she found some large fossil teeth. She had never seen anything like them before.

She showed them to her husband, Dr Gideon Mantell.

Gideon Mantell thought the teeth were very exciting. He went back to the quarry and found more teeth and some pieces of bone. He thought the fossil teeth were like those of a big lizard called an iguana. So he called the fossil Iguanodon.

He made a drawing of what he thought Iguanodon's skeleton looked like. The picture shows us that he made a mistake.

Mary Ann Mantell

Iguanodon had spikes on its thumbs

A find in a coal mine

Dr Mantell thought Iguanodon had a horn on its nose. He was wrong. No one knew this until 1877. That year, some Iguanodon fossils were found in a coal mine in Belgium.

Each skeleton had two or three 'horns'. We think they were really part of Iguanodon's thumbs.

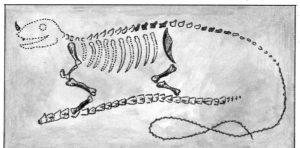

Dr Mantell's drawing of Iguanodon

The man who invented dinosaurs

The first time the word 'dinosaur' was used was in 1841.

It was invented by Dr Richard Owen, the first director of the Natural History Museum in London. It means 'terrible lizard'.

Richard Owen decided that Iguanodon and some other fossil animals that had been found all belonged in the same group. He called them all **dinosaurs**.

From that time, more and more dinosaurs were found. Even today they are still being found.

How a dinosaur becomes a fossil

1

The dead body of a dinosaur ends up at the mouth of a river. It rots and the flesh disappears.

2

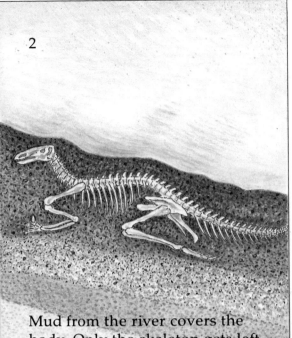

Mud from the river covers the body. Only the skeleton gets left behind. That stays because the mud holds it there.

3

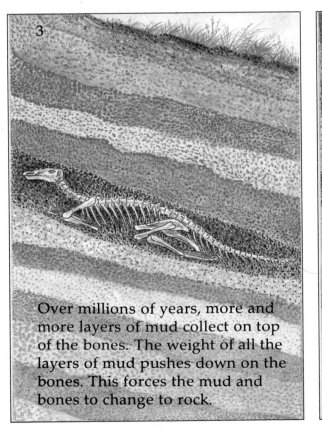

Over millions of years, more and more layers of mud collect on top of the bones. The weight of all the layers of mud pushes down on the bones. This forces the mud and bones to change to rock.

4

The mud and the bones turn into different kinds of rock. Millions of years later, a bulldozer moves the rock. It digs up the dinosaur bones.

140 million years ago

Ceratosaurus

Early mammal

8

Apatosaurus

Camptosaurus

Digging up dinosaurs

Out in the field

Fossils of dinosaurs are found in rocks. This means a quarry is a good place to find fossils. The rocks that are deepest down are also the oldest.

Dinosaur remains are only ever found in rocks of a certain age.

The rocks have to be between 65 and 230 million years old because that is when the dinosaurs lived.

Look at the picture on this page. Scientists are working in a quarry. They are taking some fossil dinosaur bones out of the rock.

Getting the bones out

The dinosaur bones are still in the rock. The scientists have to cut away the rock. They do this by using hammers and chisels, saws and drills.

Here is Ron Croucher at the Natural History Museum in London. He uses a small drill, like a dentist's, to drill away tiny bits of rock.

In this rock, there are some bones of the dinosaur Baryonyx. It will take Ron Croucher a few weeks to get all the bones safely out of the rock. Sometimes, there are very delicate fossils, which might break. These are put in acid. The acid slowly dissolves the rock but leaves the fossil behind.

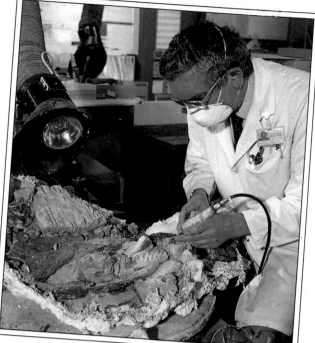

Detective work

When all the bones are out, the detective work starts.

The bones are put together like a jig-saw puzzle. Some bones are missing. So plaster ones are made to take their place.

Here the bones of a small dinosaur called Hypsilophodon have been laid out in a sand tray. This was done by Dr Angela Milner who is the expert on dinosaurs at the Natural History Museum in London.

When she has done this, she can work out what the dinosaur looked like when it was alive.

This is what we think the dinosaur Hypsilophodon looked like. Find out more about this dinosaur on pages 20–21.

Diplodocus

DINOSAUR FACTFILE

Lizard-hipped

Plants

Woody land

Dip-lod-o-kus

140 million years ago

Giraffe eating leaves

About Diplodocus

Diplodocus was too big and bulky to look anything like a giraffe. Yet, like a giraffe, it had a long neck.

Diplodocus probably used its long neck in the same way as a giraffe, to get at leaves growing at the top of tall trees.

Why did it need to do this?

It may have been because other plant-eating dinosaurs ate the leaves lower down the tree. With a long neck to help it, Diplodocus could reach food that smaller dinosaurs could not reach.

The bones in Diplodocus's neck were shaped so they locked together. These bones gave extra strength to the neck.

It also had special bones in the tail. These would have protected the delicate muscles when the tail was dragged on the ground.

The tail was long, like a whip. It could have been a dangerous weapon. Monitor lizards use their whippy tails to fight off enemies.

Diplodocus had strange teeth. Each tooth was shaped like a short pencil. Together, the teeth look like a comb. Some people think they were used to comb the leaves off trees. Diplodocus would pull its teeth along the twig and strip off the leaves.

Diplodocus had nostrils on the top of its head. Animals alive today with nostrils like these include the whales and dolphins. But we know that Diplodocus did not live in water. Elephants and other animals with trunks have nostrils on top of their head.

Perhaps Diplodocus had a trunk dangling from the top of its head. This might have helped it reach into the tree to get at the leaves.

Size and speed

Dinosaurs came in all sorts of sizes and shapes.

Brachiosaurus weighed 77 tonnes. It was about 23 metres long and 12 metres tall. Brachiosaurus would have had to plod along quite slowly. It had huge legs to support its body. It was so big that few animals could attack it.

Compsognathus was quite different. It was no bigger than a chicken. It ran fast on two legs and probably hunted small lizards. It was 60 cm long and weighed about 3 kilograms.

We think Dromiceiomimus was the fastest dinosaur.

It probably went faster than a horse can gallop. It had two long back legs – just right for taking long strides. Its stiff tail must have helped it to keep its balance as it ran. It was 3.5 metres long and weighed 100 kilograms.

Plateosaurus had broad feet and a short neck. It walked on all four legs. It was 8 metres long. It could rear up into trees so that it could reach the leaves growing at the top.

Brachiosaurus

Plateosaurus

Dromiceiomimus

Compsognathus

Fossilised footprints

The picture shows fossil dinosaur footprints. Scientists measure the space between each footprint to work out how fast the dinosaurs moved. Plant-eaters went at about 6 kilometres an hour and meat-eaters at about 16 kilometres an hour.

Sometimes, groups of footprints have been found. They all look the same, but they are different sizes.

Perhaps they were made by dinosaur families, with small young ones. Some monkeys and antelopes live in family groups, to protect and help each other. Maybe dinosaurs did this too.

Hadrosaurs on the move

Here are some ways hadrosaurs could move. Can you work out what they are doing from the way they move? The answers are upside down.

Baryonyx

DINOSAUR FACTFILE

Lizard-hipped

Meat and fish

Swampy places

Bar-ee-on-icks

124 million years ago

Brown bear waiting to catch fish

About Baryonyx

When Baryonyx was first discovered, it was nicknamed Claws – because it had amazing claws.

It may have stood on river banks, catching fish. Its long claws would be ideal for snatching fish as they swam by. Bears catch fish this way, using their claws to snatch them out of the water.

Baryonyx may have grabbed fish with its long snout. Its skull was like a crocodile's, with a spoon-shaped tip and lots of sharp teeth for gripping slippery fish. We know it ate fish because fish scales and teeth were found in its stomach.

Baryonyx was about 10 metres long. It weighed about 2 tonnes. It stood on its hind legs, and could reach up to 3 to 4 metres high.

The Baryonyx story

In January 1983, William Walker was looking for fossils in a clay pit in Surrey. He saw one in a piece of rock. He smashed the rock with his hammer. Some bits of bone fell out. Together, they made a large claw.

William Walker knew the claw was special, so his son-in-law took it to the Natural History Museum in London. Scientists there were excited. They went to the pit and found the rest of the dinosaur.

At the museum, the scientists took the most important bones from the blocks of rock. By 1986 they knew it was a new dinosaur. They named it Baryonyx walkeri. Baryonyx means 'strong claw'. The other part of its name was from William Walker, who discovered it.

Dinosaur dinners

Here is Allosaurus, a meat-eating dinosaur, attacking Camptosaurus.

Camptosaurus could be from 1.2 to 7 metres long. It weighed 500 kilograms or more. It probably crouched down to eat low-growing plants.

It escaped from danger by running fast on two legs, or by crouching down and hiding in bushes.

This one was taken by surprise by Allosaurus. Allosaurus was up to 11 metres long and weighed 1 to 2 tonnes.

Teeth

We can work out what a dinosaur ate by looking at its skull and teeth. We compare these with animals alive today.

Allosaurus

Allosaurus had over 70 sharp teeth, with tiny notches, like steak knives. These were for cutting through flesh.

Allosaurus could open its jaws very wide and bolt down large chunks of meat without chewing. Dogs and many other meat-eaters eat this way.

Camptosaurus

Camptosaurus had a long flat head and many teeth, with ridges on them.

It had a horny beak to cut leaves from plants. There was a wide groove in its mouth. This may have held a long tongue which it used for reaching out for twigs to eat.

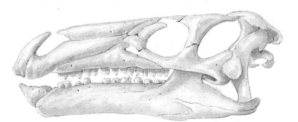

Stones in the stomach

Very smooth, rounded stones have been found in fossil dinosaurs, just where the stomach would have been. These stones helped in digesting food. We know that some birds and crocodiles swallow stones to help break up their food. We think dinosaurs swallowed these stones on purpose.

Hypsilophodon

DINOSAUR FACTFILE

Bird-hipped | Plants | Swampy places

Hip-si-low-fo-don

120 million years ago

Gazelle on the African plains

About Hypsilophodon

Hypsilophodon belonged to a group of dinosaurs called the hypsilophodontids. From fossils, we know these were around for 100 million years.

Hypsilophodon was about 2 metres long. It lived a life like the gazelles of today.

It ate plants and lived in herds. It had long legs like a gazelle and a stiff tail which kept the head and body balanced when it ran.

It used its horny beak to bite its food. The teeth were self-sharpening. They were sharpened by the top and bottom teeth working against each other.

Who am I?

Here is a dinosaur, telling a story about life millions of years ago. You have to work out which dinosaur it is. The answer is on page 47.

'The herd starts the day roaming over the plains, looking for good grazing. I stray away from the herd to nibble some delicious magnolia bushes. My horny beak snips the flowers off the tree.

'Suddenly, there is a loud roar behind me. Turning round I see a huge Tyrannosaurus towering above me – its teeth gleaming in the sun.

'I'm scared, but I turn to face it. To run away now would be dangerous, so I hope my neck frill will make me look bigger. The Tyrannosaurus stops in his tracks. I raise my head so he sees my long, sharp horns. He decides to charge. I am ready to fight to the death, but just then I hear some friendly noises.

'It's the herd. They have come to my rescue. Together we make a half-moon shape, presenting our horns head on. The Tyrannosaurus decides that there are too many of us to fight, and he moves away.

'Tomorrow I promise to stay with the herd and not stray away!'

Dinosaur heads

Pachycephalosaurus probably used its head for fighting.

Male bighorn sheep fight each other in the mating season.

Why special heads?

Many dinosaurs had large crests, horns and weird frills around their heads. Dinosaurs with heads like these were mostly plant-eaters.

If we look at the large plant-eating animals today, what do we see?

Deer have antlers. Cattle, antelopes and goats all have horns on their heads. They use them for fighting, mainly with each other. The males do this in the breeding season.

Dinosaurs may have used their horns this way. Perhaps they lived in groups, like sheep. Maybe there was a leader – perhaps the strongest one.

Bonehead

Pachycephalosaurus had a thick head.

There was an extra thick bone around its skull. This bone would have protected the head like a motor cyclists' crash helmet.

The males probably fought by banging their heads together.

Bighorn sheep from North America do the same thing using their horns. Males fight with each other.

They do not kill each other. The strongest wins the fight by pushing the other away with his horns.

The winner then chooses the females he wants as mates.

Some dinosaurs, like Chasmosaurus, had frills around their necks.

The frilled lizard is found in Australia.

Frills

One group of dinosaurs have frills of bone around the neck. They could have been used in lots of ways.

Perhaps the dinosaurs used them as signals to show off to each other. They may have been very colourful.

Perhaps the frill helped each dinosaur recognise other dinosaurs of the same kind as itself.

Maybe the frill made the dinosaur look bigger, to frighten enemies. It might have been a shield to protect the dinosaur in fights.

We can get a clue from the frilled lizard. Most of the time this lizard keeps its frill folded, like an umbrella. If it is frightened it opens its frill. It stands still and faces its enemy. The frill makes it look terrifying and a lot bigger.

Hadrosaurs

Hadrosaurs were plant-eating dinosaurs. Sometimes, they are called duck-bills. Scientists think that they lived together in herds.

They had amazing crests and shapes on their heads. Perhaps they used these to signal to each other.

One kind of hadrosaur had a fleshy balloon on its head. It blew the balloon up with air. It might have used this to make a loud noise to call to other hadrosaurs.

Other animals, like frogs and some monkeys, do this. Perhaps some dinosaurs were noisy creatures.

Iguanodon

Megalosaurus

Polacanthus

Skin and blood

Stegosaurus was a large plant-eating dinosaur. It could not move very fast.

It probably had few enemies because it had so many spikes to protect it. It also had many large, bony plates on its back.

We are not sure what these were for, but they must have been good protection. There were long, dagger-like spikes on its tail. These would have been useful, too.

It was quite a prickly meal, even for a big meat-eating dinosaur.

Warm blood, cold blood

Mammals and birds are warm blooded. Their body heat stays the same, however cold or hot the weather is. They have fur or feathers to help with this.

Insects, fish, amphibians and reptiles are cold blooded. They do not have fur or feathers. They become warm in warm weather, and cool when the weather cools down.

Some people think the dinosaurs were warm blooded. But they probably had scaly skin, with no fur or feathers.

Stegosaurus might have used the plates on its back to control its body heat. If it stood with the plates facing the sun, these would warm up and warm the whole body.

If some dinosaurs did control their body temperature then these might have been warm blooded.

Deinonychus

DINOSAUR FACTFILE

Lizard-hipped

Meat

Open land

Die-non-e-kus

110 million years ago

A pack of wolves hunting

About Deinonychus

Deinonychus was a small dinosaur. Fossils show us it was a fast, brainy and ferocious animal. It was about 1.5 metres tall and up to 3 metres long. It weighed about 75 kilograms – about the same as a man.

It probably lived in packs, like wolves. Wolves can kill very large animals, as there are so many in a pack. They chase an animal such as a moose. When the moose is so tired that it cannot run any more, the wolves tear it to pieces.

Deinonychus ran fast on its hind legs. Its stiff tail helped it to keep its balance. It used its big eyes to look for food.

Deinonychus probably held onto its prey with its front claws and kicked it with its back ones. Its sharp teeth pointed backwards and helped it grip its prey. Even large dinosaurs would be in danger from a pack of Deinonychus.

Fossils like Deinonychus made people change their minds about dinosaurs. They had thought all dinosaurs were slow and lumbering. Now we think some were fast and intelligent, with large brains. Some may have been warm blooded. They probably lived like mammals today.

Breeding and babies

Like many other animals, dinosaurs changed the way they behaved in the breeding season.

This behaviour is called **courtship**. Males might fight with each other. The females would choose the winner, because he would be fitter and healthier than the others.

Males and females might have used special sounds to call to each other. Or they may have used bright colours to signal to each other that they were ready to breed.

The male agama lizard, from Africa, turns bright colours in the breeding season. He uses these colours to warn other males: 'Keep out of my territory'. The agama also uses the colours to attract females.

Colourful dinosaurs

We think some dinosaurs were as colourful as lizards and birds. We will probably never know if we are right. But the world of the dinosaurs might have been very colourful.

Courtship

After courtship birds make nests to lay their eggs in.

Flamingos nest together in huge colonies. They build nests made from mud. All the nests are exactly the same distance apart. There is something special about this distance. Each nest is just out of reach of its neighbour.

A flamingo sits on its egg. The heat from the bird's body keeps the egg warm. After a number of days, the young bird hatches. It is fed and looked after by its parents.

Fossil nests

Maiasaura was a dinosaur that made nests. Fossil nests have been found, all the same distance apart, like flamingos' nests.

This distance is the exact length of a Maiasaura. We think Maiasaura took care of its nest and used the heat from rotting plants to keep its eggs warm. Crocodiles do this.

Eggs

Some fossil eggs were found in the Gobi Desert in Mongolia. A dinosaur called Protoceratops laid its eggs in the sand and left them to hatch.

A dinosaur called Oviraptor (which means 'egg thief') would dig up the eggs and use its strong jaws and beak to crush and eat them.

Amnion

Here is a reptile egg. Dinosaurs' eggs were the same. All eggs have a layer inside called the amnion. Birds have this. So do mammals – although they have live young. Its amnion protects the growing baby. It is one thing which connects us to the dinosaurs.

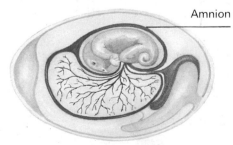

Amnion

Triceratops

DINOSAUR FACTFILE

Bird-hipped Plants Woody land

Try-serra-tops

70–65 million years ago

An African rhinoceros

About Triceratops

Triceratops was a large plant-eating dinosaur. It weighed 5.5 tonnes and was 9 metres long. It had three horns on its head.

It probably ate mainly palm leaves. These are quite tough, so Triceratops had a very sharp beak to bite off the leaves.

It had a big muscle connecting its horny frill to its jaw. This shows it must have had a sharp, strong bite.

Triceratops's teeth worked like the blades of a pair of scissors. It could snip pieces of leaves off easily, ready for swallowing.

As Triceratops ate this tough food, its teeth would have worn down and fallen out. New teeth would have grown instead.

In some ways Triceratops was like the rhinoceros.

It was a plant-eater, like the rhinoceros. There is a difference, though. Rhinoceroses live alone, but so many Triceratops fossils have been found together that we think they lived in herds.

Triceratops must have had many ways of escaping from the big meat-eating dinosaurs. If it lived in herds, there would be safety in numbers. If there was danger, it could run away.

Some people think it could have run at 48 kilometres an hour. It could also have used its long horns to defend itself.

The big bony frill around its neck would have made a good shield, and it had sharp teeth for biting.

Dinosaurs alive today?

The dinosaurs all died out 65 million years ago. But there are plenty of other reptiles alive today. These include lizards, snakes, crocodiles, alligators, tortoises and turtles.

There is also the tuatara, which lives in New Zealand. These were alive when dinosaurs ruled the Earth.

They looked exactly the same then as today. Some people call the tuatara a **living fossil**.

Crocodiles are more closely related to the dinosaurs than any other reptile. They were around at the time of the dinosaurs. But they looked different from crocodiles now.

tuatara

tortoise

lizard

crocodile

The Archaeopteryx story

Some people think that one group of dinosaurs lives on. They think that group developed into birds.

They think this because of this fossil. It is called Archaeopteryx. It was found in Germany. It looked like a small dinosaur called a coelosaur.

It had teeth and claws like a dinosaur. But there was also the imprint of feathers in the rock.

It looked like a dinosaur with feathers. It seems that it was part dinosaur and part bird.

It was not good at flying. It may have used its wings to flutter off the ground chasing after insects. Perhaps it used its claws to climb trees. It would then glide down from the tree. It was probably warm blooded. Birds today are warm blooded and use their feathers to keep their body heat in and the cold out.

Monster myths

You must have heard of the Loch Ness monster. There are stories of another animal like it, in West Africa.

Sometimes, people say these animals are dinosaurs. But they both live in water, so they cannot be. The Loch Ness monster is supposed to look like a plesiosaur – a big swimming reptile that lived in the sea.

Gallimimus

DINOSAUR FACTFILE

Lizard-hipped

Plants and meat

Open land

Gallee-mee-mus

90-70 million years ago

Ostrich in Africa

About Gallimimus

This dinosaur was 4 metres long. It may have lived a life like an ostrich, on the open plains. With its long neck and large eyes, it could spot danger a long way off and then run away.

Gallimimus's whole body was built for fast running – it was one of the fastest dinosaurs on earth.

The skull was very light, with no teeth. Its legs were very long. The tail would have been held straight out to help it balance.

Like ostriches today, it probably ate a mixture of many kinds of foods, such as fruit, leaves, seeds, insects and lizards.

Its fossils were found in southern Mongolia.

What's left behind

Fossils are mainly the hard part of animals. The flesh and soft parts rot away. Imagine in a million years' time, what we might have left behind.

What things from this picture would disappear and what might be found? What would people think about how we lived from just these items? (The answers are on page 47.)

An old bicycle wheel

A plastic lemonade bottle

A plastic shopping bag

A fast food container

A left-over bit of Sunday lunch

A drink can

Dinosaur deaths

Some people use the word 'dinosaur' in the wrong way. They call someone a dinosaur if they will not listen to new ideas or change their ways. They think the dinosaurs were like that.

But that's not true. There were dinosaurs for over 160 million years – over thirty times longer than people have been around.

They changed, too. Some kinds lived early on. Different kinds were alive much later. So why do people use the word dinosaur in the wrong way?

It's because about 65 million years ago all the dinosaurs died out. We do not know if they all died suddenly or over a long time.

But we do know that whatever killed the dinosaurs also killed many other kinds of animals. So it's unfair to say that only the dinosaurs were unable to change, when there were other groups that died out too.

Look below to see who were the winners and who were the losers at this time on Earth.

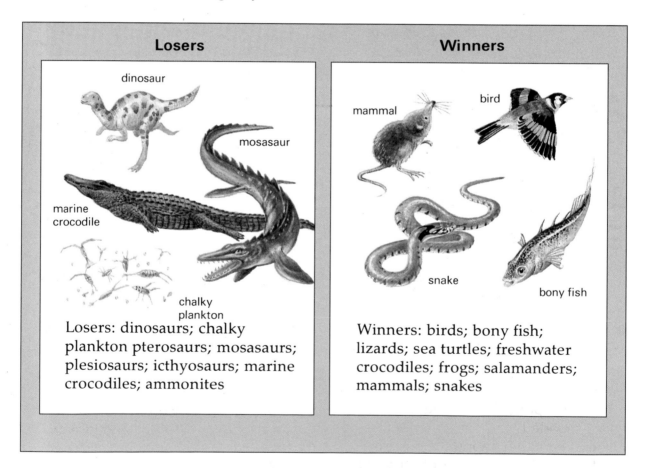

Losers

dinosaur

mosasaur

marine crocodile

chalky plankton

Losers: dinosaurs; chalky plankton pterosaurs; mosasaurs; plesiosaurs; icthyosaurs; marine crocodiles; ammonites

Winners

mammal

bird

snake

bony fish

Winners: birds; bony fish; lizards; sea turtles; freshwater crocodiles; frogs; salamanders; mammals; snakes

Winners and losers
–65 million years ago

All these animals were alive at the same time 65 million years ago. The ones on the left became extinct. The ones on the right survived. Why did some die out and not others?

All kinds of reasons have been worked out. Some are rubbish. That's because they are only about dinosaurs – yet many other animals died out too. Most scientists think it was because the world's climate changed. This might have happened in one of these ways.

The first idea is this.

1 A huge meteorite hit the Earth. It sent dust and water vapour into the air.

2 There was so much dust it blotted out the sun's heat. The climate changed.

3 The new climate meant not so many plants grew. There was less to eat.

Larger animals need more food than the smaller ones. There were fewer and fewer of them. They died out.

The smaller animals could eat lots of different things. They could find enough to eat. They survived.

The second idea is this.

1 The climate was warm and wet. There were lots of tropical plants.

2 The new climate was cooler. The plants changed to woodland plants.

3 This kind of environment was right for some animals.

But it was too cold for dinosaurs and the other big reptiles. They died out. The warm-blooded birds and mammals could keep warm enough to survive – and the smaller reptiles could hibernate when it got too cold.

Thanks to the dinosaurs

We will probably never know what happened. But we should be thankful the dinosaurs became extinct. Why?

Because until the dinosaurs went, mammals were only small, shrew-like animals. When the dinosaurs had gone, they became larger and different and much more important. One kind of mammal developed into humans. Who knows what may have happened if the dinosaurs had never died out?

70 million years ago

Tyrannosaurus

Ankylosaurus

Parasaurolophus

Dinosaur puzzles

Time travel quiz
Here are four different pictures of times dinosaurs and other animals were around on Earth. They are in the wrong order.

What you have to do is to rearrange them. Put them in order of time, with the earliest picture first. Use the clues in this book to help you. (The answers are on page 47.)

A

B

C

D

Swimming and flying
Dinosaurs could not swim or fly. But there were other reptiles at the time that could.

The pterosaurs were flying reptiles. Some were huge. We do not know if they flapped their wings, or if they could only glide.

The plesiosaurs and icthyosaurs lived in the sea and swam using flippers. the plesiosaurs had long necks. Some people believe the Loch Ness monster is a plesiosaur. Icthyosaurs looked like dolphins.

These reptiles ruled the air and sea. Dinosaurs ruled the land.

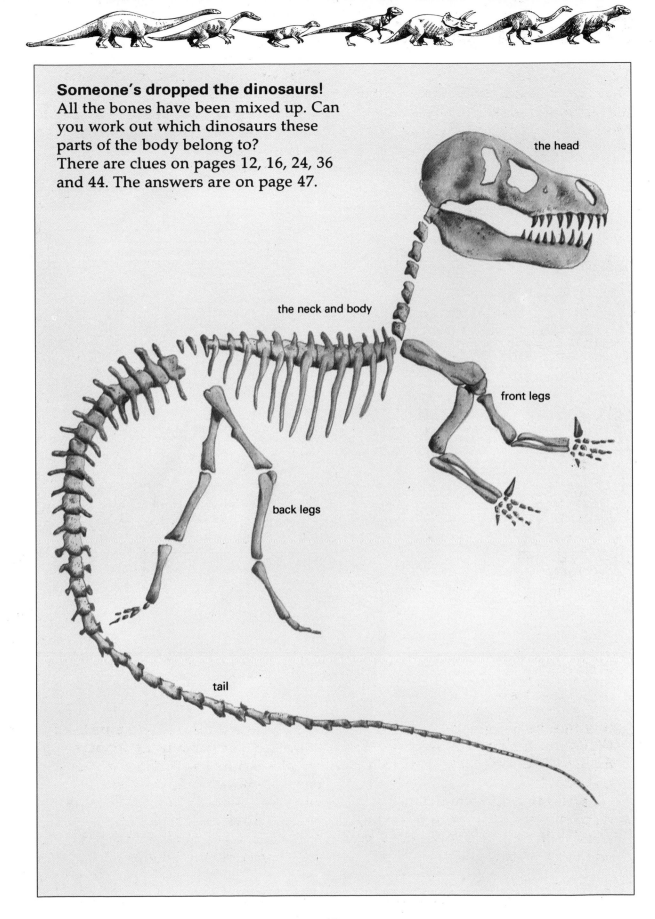

Someone's dropped the dinosaurs!
All the bones have been mixed up. Can you work out which dinosaurs these parts of the body belong to?
There are clues on pages 12, 16, 24, 36 and 44. The answers are on page 47.

the head

the neck and body

front legs

back legs

tail

Tyrannosaurus

DINOSAUR FACTFILE

Lizard-hipped

Meat

Woody land

Tie-ran-oh-saw-rus

70–65 million years ago

Tiger

About Tyrannosaurus

Tyrannosaurus was one of the biggest meat-eating dinosaurs. It was 12 metres long. It was as tall as the tallest giraffe at 5.6 metres high. It weighed as much as an African elephant at 6.4 tonnes.

The skull of Tyrannosaurus was 1.2 metres long and its jaws were so wide it could have swallowed a person whole.

Tyrannosaurus might have lived a bit like the tiger.

A tiger hunts its prey by creeping up on it. Then it leaps. It uses its teeth to kill. We do not know whether Tyrannosaurus hunted this way. It certainly had big teeth.

Some people think that Tyrannosaurus could not run. It could only walk quickly. So perhaps it could not chase other dinosaurs and kill them. Perhaps it ate the remains of dinosaurs that were already dead. It could have been a scavenger, not a hunter at all!

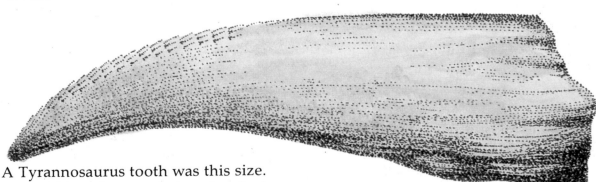

A Tyrannosaurus tooth was this size. Its saw-like edge was for cutting flesh.

Solutions and answers

Answers to pages 2 and 3

Were all dinosaurs big?

No, not all dinosaurs were big. The biggest, such as Brachiosaurus, were huge – as high as a house. At the other end of the scale was Compsognathus, which was the size of a chicken. Pages 14–15 tell you more about the sizes of dinosaurs.

Could any dinosaurs swim?

None of the dinosaurs found so far could swim. People used to think that the very big plant-eaters, such as Brachiosaurus and Diplodocus, had to live in water. This was because their bodies were so huge they could only be supported by water. We now know this to be untrue. No dinosaur would have been able to swim.

Did any dinosaurs fly?

No dinosaurs could fly. There probably would not have been any room in the air if they did! There were a lot of flying reptiles around. These were the pterosaurs.

Pterosaurs had a membrane of skin which stretched between the legs and arms. This made their wings. One of the biggest was Quetzalcoatlus. It had a wingspan of 15 metres. It was probably the biggest flying animal that ever lived. But it was not a dinosaur.

Are there any dinosaurs alive today?

No, certainly not. Stories of monsters like the Loch Ness monster make some people think that dinosaurs live on somewhere. But the only dinosaurs around today are in stories and films! Pages 34–35 tell you more.

Has anyone ever seen a live dinosaur?

No. No human being has ever seen a living dinosaur. The dinosaurs died out 65 million years ago. People did not even appear on the Earth until four million years ago. So they could never have met each other.

Were all dinosaurs stupid?

No. Some had quite small brains. Stegosaurus had a brain the size of a walnut. Others had quite large brains. Deinonychus had a big brain and large eyes. It needed a big brain to control its body when hunting.

So it would be wrong to say that all dinosaurs were stupid.

Were they all slow and lumbering?

Some dinosaurs might have been quite slow. Many people think of Tyrannosaurus as a deadly killer. But it could probably only walk at 6.5 kilometres an hour.

Other dinosaurs such as Triceratops could have been able to run at more than 45 kilometres an hour, even though it was very large. Some, such as Struthiomimus, may have run as fast as 50 kilometres per hour.

They were certainly not all slow and lumbering.

Were any dinosaurs colourful?

We don't know. That's because the skin of dinosaurs is hardly ever left behind, and when it is, the colour never stays. But many animals alive today are colourful. Therefore it is likely that some dinosaurs were brightly coloured and others were not. Look at pages 30–31 to find out more.

Were dinosaurs warm blooded or cold blooded?

Dinosaurs were reptiles. Reptiles today are cold blooded. So until the 1970s, most scientists thought dinosaurs could only be cold blooded. But since then dinosaur fossils have been found which